Dear Parents and Educators,

Welcome to Penguin Young Readers! As parents and educators, you know that each child develops at their own pace—in terms of speech, critical thinking, and, of course, reading. Penguin Young Readers recognizes this fact. As a result, each Penguin Young Readers book is assigned a traditional easy-to-read level (1–4) as well as a Guided Reading Level (A–P). Both of these systems will help you choose the right book for your child. Please refer to the back of each book for specific leveling information. Penguin Young Readers features esteemed authors and illustrators, stories about favorite characters, fascinating nonfiction, and more!

Peter Rabbit™ 2
Bunny Trouble

LEVEL 2
GUIDED READING LEVEL I

This book is perfect for a **Progressing Reader** who:
- can figure out unknown words by using picture and context clues;
- can recognize beginning, middle, and ending sounds;
- can make and confirm predictions about what will happen in the text; and
- can distinguish between fiction and nonfiction.

Here are some **activities** you can do during and after reading this book:
- Problem/Solutions: The problem in this story is that Peter doesn't want Thomas and Bea to forget about him. What does Peter do to make sure this doesn't happen?
- Make Connections: Even though they are all bunnies, Peter and his friends are special in their own unique ways. How are your friends different from you? What makes them special?

Remember, sharing the love of reading with a child is the best gift you can give!

D1055802

PENGUIN YOUNG READERS
An Imprint of Penguin Random House LLC, New York

Penguin supports copyright. Copyright fuels creativity, encourages diverse voices,
promotes free speech, and creates a vibrant culture. Thank you for buying an
authorized edition of this book and for complying with copyright laws by
not reproducing, scanning, or distributing any part of it in any form
without permission. You are supporting writers and allowing Penguin to
continue to publish books for every reader.

Published in the United States of America in 2020 by Penguin Young Readers, an imprint of
Penguin Random House LLC, New York. Manufactured in China.

Visit us online at www.penguinrandomhouse.com.

ISBN 9780241410868

10 9 8 7 6 5 4 3 2 1

PETER RABBIT 2

BUNNY TROUBLE

Peter lives in a garden in the country.

The country is a good place for a bunny.
There are trees and flowers, and fruit and vegetables to eat.

Peter shares the garden with lots of friends.
His family lives there, too.
Peter's sisters are named Flopsy, Mopsy, and Cotton-tail.

Peter's cousin is named
Benjamin.
Peter and Benjamin
are best friends.

The garden belongs
to Bea and Thomas.
They love rabbits!

10

Bea and Thomas try to look after Peter and his family.

Bea and Thomas have some news.
They are getting married.

All of the bunnies
go to the wedding.
It is a happy day.

Bea likes to make paintings of Peter and his friends. They are very good.

One day, Thomas helps Bea make her paintings into a book.

Everyone loves Bea's book.
Now Bea and Thomas are very busy.
They spend lots of time in the city.

"Don't forget me," says Peter.

17

Peter wants to find out more about the city. Perhaps he will like the city better than the countryside.

19

When he gets there, the bunny sees that the city is not like the country!

The streets are dark and dirty.

Peter meets a rabbit called Barnabas. He asks Peter to join his team.

Barnabas wants the bunny to help him steal some fruit.

24

Peter is
not sure.

25

The plan sounds fun,
but Peter is not a bad bunny.
He does not want to do
bad things.

Just in time, Peter's sisters and Benjamin find him.

Even Thomas has come. "Let's go home," says Thomas.

Peter is back in the country. He is happy to be with his family.

Peter Rabbit loves adventure.
And great news—he's about to find one in the city!
What trouble will he get into this time?

LEVEL 1

Emergent Reader (Guided Reading Levels A–D)

LEVEL 2

GUIDED READING LEVEL

E F G H I

Progressing Reader
• Longer sentences
• Simple dialogue
• Picture and context clues
• More in-depth plot development
• Nonfiction and fiction

LEVEL 3

Transitional Reader (Guided Reading Levels J–M)

LEVEL 4

Fluent Reader (Guided Reading Levels N–P)

*Penguin Young Readers are leveled by independent reviewers applying the standards developed by Irene Fo
and Gay Su Pinnell in *Matching Books to Readers: Using Leveled Books in Guided Reading*, Heinemann 1999.

ISBN 978-0-241-41086-8

5 0 4 9 9 >

9 780241 410868

$4.99 US

PENGUIN YOUNG READERS
Visit us at penguinyoungreaders.com

Time

Today	*jīntiān*	[jin-tee'en]
Tomorrow	*míngtiān*	[ming tee'en]
Yesterday	*zuótiān*	[dz'wo(r) tee'en]
The day after tomorrow	*hòutiān*	[hoe tee'en]
The day before yesterday	*qiántiān*	[chee'an tee'en]
Now	*xiànzài*	[shen-dz'eye]

Place

At (or '**to be at**')	*zài*	[dz'eye]

(Tom is at the hotel – *Tom zài fàndiàn)*

7. Question Words

Although there is some slightly more complicated grammar surrounding the use of question words, in Basic Chinese, these are relatively easy to use. In general, the question words can be added before the verb or end of the sentence.
Note that 'where' is usually added at the end and "how" is added before the verb.

What?	*Shénme?*	[shuh-muh]
Where?	*Nǎ lǐ?*	[nah-lee]
Who?	*Shuí?*	[sh'way]
(*Shéi?* [shay] in the North, including Beijing)		
Why?	*Wéi shénme?*	[way shuh-muh]
When?	*Shénme shíhou?*	[shuh-muh sh'r-hoe]
How?	*Zěnme?*	[dzuh-muh]

Examples

How do you eat this?	*Zhèigè zěnme chī?*	[jay-guh dzuh-muh ch'r]
What does that mean?	*Shénme yì sī?*	[shuh-muh ee-suh]
Who is coming?	*Shuí lái?*	[sh'way lie]
Why don't you like him / her?	*Nǐ wéi shénme bú xǐhuān tā?*	[knee way shuh-muh boo shee-hwan tah]
Where are we going? ("We go where?")	*Wǒ men qù nǎ lǐ?*	[wo(r) men choo nah-lee]
What do you want? ("You want what?")	*(Nǐ) yào shénme?*	[knee yow shuh-muh]
Who is this? ("This is who?")	*Zhèi shì shuí?*	[jay sh'r sh'way]
What do you want to drink? ("You drink what?")	*Nǐ hē shénme?*	[knee huh shuh-muh]
When do you want to go?	*Nǐ shénme shíhòu yào qù?*	[knee shuh-muh sh'r-hoe yow chew]
Where is the Forbidden City? (= *Gùgōng*)	*Gùgōng zài nǎ lǐ?*	[goo-gong dz'eye nah-lee]

14

8. Numbers and Counting

General
Numbers in Chinese are extremely easy if you memorise the first 10.

(0	*líng*	[ling])
1	*yī*	[ee]
2	*èr, liǎng*	[ar], [lee'ang]
3	*sān*	[san]
4	*sì*	[suh]
5	*wǔ*	[woo]
6	*liù*	[leo]
7	*qī*	[chee]
8	*bā*	[bah]
9	*jiǔ*	[j'yo]
10	*shí*	[sh'r]

A note about the number 2: You will see that there are two words for the number 2 – 'èr' and 'liǎng'.
Èr: Used when counting or just stating numbers, e.g. *Xiànzài shì qī diǎn èr shí wǔ* – Now it is 7:25 (A brief section on 'Telling the Time' will follow).
Liǎng: Used when stating how many of something, e.g. *Yào liǎng wǎn mǐ fàn* – I want 2 bowls of rice.

Above 10, the numbers are simply stated as follows:

12	*shí èr*	[sh'r ar]	"ten two"
15	*shí wǔ*	[sh'r woo]	"ten five"
20	*èr shí*	[ar sh'r]	"two ten"
23	*èr shí sān*	[ar sh'r san]	"two ten three"
30	*sān shí*	[san sh'r]	"three ten"
78	*qī shí bā*	[chee sh'r bah]	"seven ten eight"

100	*yī bǎi*	[ee bye]	
124	*yī bǎi èr shí sì*		"One hundred two ten four"
648	*liù bǎi sì shí bā*		"Six hundred four ten eight"

1000	*yī qiān*	[ee chee'en]

Easy Practice
Work out these numbers in Chinese: 150, 725, 932.

Stating how many

When stating the number of something in Chinese, a word is normally added after the number, so that when asked how many, the answer is not 1 or 5 etc. It is 1 thing, or 5 bottles, or 15 tickets etc.

Although you will learn more specific words for different objects if you spend any time in China, the most useful word that can be added and generally used for most things is '*gè*'.

1 thing	*yī gè*	[ee guh]
10 things	*shí gè*	[sh'r guh]

Examples

I want one	*Yào yī gè*	[yow ee-guh]

Three tickets *Sān gè (piào)* [san-guh pee'ow]
 i.e. the proper word used when saying how many tickets is '*zhāng*' but '*gè*' is understood in context.
 (Note that the actual word for ticket is '*piào*' but does not normally need to be stated at ticket booths – since it is already obvious what you are asking for).

Six cans of sprite *Liù gè xuěbì* [leo-guh sh'way-bee]
 i.e. the proper word used for can is '*tīng*' but '*gè*' is understood

Two bowls of rice *Liǎng gè mǐ fàn* [lee'ang-guh mee-fan]
 i.e. the proper word used for bowl is '*wǎn*' but '*gè*' is understood

1st, 2nd, 3rd etc.

For ordinal numbers, all you need is to precede the number with '*di*' and follow it
with '*gè*'.

1st	*dì yī gè*	[dee ee guh]
2nd	*dì èr gè*	[dee ar guh]
3rd	*dì sān gè*	[dee san-guh]
25th	*dì èr shí wǔ gè*	[dee ar-sh'r woo-guh]

Example
At the 2nd traffic light, turn right   *Dì èr gè hóng lǜ dēng yòuguǎi*
[dee ar guh hong lieu dung yo gwai]

Telling the time

To do this, just add the word '*diǎn*' [dee'en] after the hour to denote "o'clock". Note that the format for times in Chinese includes "o'clock" no matter what the time is.

1:00	*yī diǎn*	[ee dee'en]	"1 o'clock"
1:25	*yī diǎn èr shí wǔ*		"1 'o'clock' 25"
7:50	*qī diǎn wǔ shí*		"7 'o'clock' 50"

and so on...

To say 'half past' an hour, simply say the hour plus '*diǎn bàn*' [dee'en ban]. (ban = half, so to say 4:30, we really say "4 o'clock half")

4:30	*sì diǎn bàn*	[suh dee'en ban]	"4 o'clock half"

Asking: **What time is it?** *Jǐ diǎn le?* [jee dee'en luh]

Easy Practice
Work out these times as above:
6:30, 9:45, 3:10.

18

9. Situational Chinese

In a Taxi

Go to...	*qù*	[chew]
Go (this way)	*zǒu*	[dz'oh]

(This can be used to say which way to go – e.g. *Zǒu gāo sù* – Go on the expressway)

Turn right	*yòuguǎi*	[yo gwai]
Turn left	*zuǒguǎi*	[dz'wo(r) gwai]
Go straight	*yī zhí zǒu*	[ee-juh-zoh]

Stop the car (This is where I get out)	*tíng chē*	[ting chuh]

Here	*zhèi lǐ*	[juh-lee]
There	*nà lǐ*	[nah-lee]

Turn around or **Do a u-turn**	*diào tóu*	[dee'ow toe]

(At the) traffic light	*hóng lǜ dēng*	[hong lieu dung]

Up ahead	*qiánmiàn*	[chee'an mee'en]

Go faster	*kuài yī diǎn*	[kwai ee dee'en]
Slow down	*màn yī diǎn*	[man ee dee'en]

For Beijing:

2nd Ring Rd	*Èrhuán*	[ar-hwan]
3rd Ring Rd	*Sānhuán*	[san-hwan]
4th Ring Rd	*Sìhuán*	[suh-hwan]

Asking for Directions:

Where is (Xidan)?	*(Xīdān) zài nǎ lǐ?*	[shee-dan dz'eye nah-lee]
To get to Guomao, **how should I go?**	*Dào Guómào* *zěnme zǒu?*	[dow gwo(r)-mao dz'uh-muh dz'oh]

Example of a Simple Journey:

Hello. Go to Andingmen...	*Nǐ hǎo. Qù Āndìngmén ...*
Go on the 2nd Ring Road.	*Zǒu Èrhuán.*
At the lights, turn right,	*Hóng lǜ dēng, yòuguǎi,*
** then turn left.**	*ránhòu zuǒguǎi.*
Ok stop here. Thank you.	*Ok, zhè lǐ tíng chē.. Xiè xiè.*

19

In a Restaurant

(If travelling to Beiing, I am creating a list of some of the best restaurants and bars here: http://pinterest.com/jimmcg1/best-beijing-restaurants-bars. More will be added as time goes on).

Getting a Table

'Persons', places	*wèi*	[way]
(How many people?	*Jǐ wèi?*	[jee way])
(3 / 4 people	*Sān / Sì wèi*	[san / suh way])

Food

Beef	*niú ròu*	[n'yo roe]
Chicken	*jī ròu*	[jee roe]
Lamb	*yáng ròu*	[yahng roe]
Pork	*zhū ròu*	[joo roe]
Fish	*yú*	[yew]
Vegetables	*shū cài*	[shoo ts'eye]
Vegetarian dishes	*sù cài*	[soo ts'eye]
(I'm a vegetarian	*Wǒ chī sù*	[wo(r) ch'r soo])
Rice	*mǐ fàn*	[mee fan]

Ordering

We want {1 / 2 / 3...}	*Yào {yī / liǎng / sān...}*
Bring {1 / 2 / 3...}	*Lái {yī / liǎng / sān...}*
Bring another {1 / 2...}	*Zài lái [dz'eye lie] {yī / liǎng...}*

Bowl	*wǎn*	[wan]
Glass	*bēi*	[bay]
Bottle	*píng*	[ping]
Anything else	*gè*	[guh]

Useful Restaurant Language

Waiter	*fúwùyuán*	[foo'oo-yoo'an]
Check / Bill	*mǎi dān*	[my dan]

   (i.e. to request the check / bill: *"Fúwùyuán! Mǎi dān!"*)

Knife and fork   *dāo chā*   [dow cha]
   (Do you have a knife and fork? – *Yǒu dāo chā ma?*)

Chopsticks   *kuàizǐ*   [kwai dzuh]
   (I can't use chopsticks – *Wǒ bú huì yòng kuàizǐ*)

Spicy   *là de*   [laah duh]
   (Is this one spicy? – *Zhèigè shì là de ma?*)
   (I don't want it spicy – *Bú yào là de*)

Menu   *cài dān*   [ts'eye dan]
(Do you have an English menu? – *Yǒu yīng wén cài dān ma?*)

Example of a simple visit:

"Hello, how many people?"	*"Nǐ hǎo, jǐ wèi?"*
4 people.	*Sì wèi.*

Waiter!	*Fúwùyuán!*

I want 1 kung pao chicken,	*Yào yīgè gōng bǎo jī ding,*
2 shredded potato dishes.	*liǎnggè tǔ dòu sī.*
	[gong bao jee ding; too doe suh]

Bring 4 bowls of rice.	*Lái sì wǎn mǐ fàn.*

Do you have beer?	*Yǒu pí jiǔ ma?*
Ok, bring 4 glasses of beer.	*Ok, lái sì bēi pí jiǔ.*

Do you have a knife and fork?	*Yǒu dāo chā ma?*

Thank you.	*Xiè xiè.*

Waiter! Check, please!	*Fúwùyuán! Mǎi dān!*

Thank you.	*Xiè xiè.*

In a Bar

(If travelling to Beiing, I am creating a list of some of the best restaurants and bars here: http://pinterest.com/jimmcg1/best-beijing-restaurants-bars. More will be added as time goes on).

Ordering

I want (no.) bottles of (beer)	*Yào (no.) píng (píjiǔ)*	[yow … ping pee-j'yo]
Bring (no.) glasses of (draught beer)	*Lái (no.) bēi (zhāpí)*	[lie … bay jaah-pee]
Bring another {1 / 2}	*Zài lái {yī / liǎng} gè*	[dz'eye lie ee-guh / lee'ang guh]

Numbers (when ordering)

1. *yī* [ee], **2.** *liǎng* [lee'ang], **3.** *sān* [san], **4.** *sì* [suh], **5.** *wǔ* [woo], **6.** *liù* [leo], **7.** *qī* [chee], **8.** *bā* [bah], **9.** *jiǔ* [j'yo], **10.** *shí* [sh'r]

Drinks

<u>Alcoholic:</u>
beer – *píjiǔ* [pee-j'yo], **draught beer** – *zhāpí* [jaah-pee], **white wine** – *bái pútáojiǔ* [bye poo-tao-j'yo], **red wine** – *hóng pútáojiǔ* [hong poo-tao-j'yo], **rice wine** – *báijiǔ* [bye-j'yo]

<u>Non-alcoholic:</u>
(mineral) water – *kuàngquán shuǐ* [koo'ung-choo'an shway], **coke** – *kě lè* [kuh-luh], **sprite** – *xuěbì* [shway-bee], **orange juice** – *chéng zhī* [chung j'r], **coffee** – *kā fēi* [kah-fay], **tea** – *chá* [chaah], **iced tea** – *bīng chá* [bing-chaah]

I don't want ice	*Bú yào bīng*	[boo yow bing]
Do you have cold ones?	*Yǒu bīng de ma?*	[yo bing-duh ma]

In a Shop

Price & Bargaining

How much is it?	*Duō shǎo qián?*	[dwo(r) shao chee'en]
100 Yuan	*Yī bǎi yuán / kuài*	[ee-bye yoo'an / kwai]
It's too expensive	*Tài guì*	[tie gway]
I'll give you 80 Yuan	*Gěi nǐ bā shí kuài*	[gay knee bah sh'r kwai]

Size

Do you have bigger?	*Yǒu dà yī diǎn de ma?*	[yo daah ee dee'en ma]
Do you have smaller?	*Yǒu xiǎo yī diǎn de ma?*	[yo sh'yow ee dee'en ma]

Making Your Purchase

I want this	*Yào zhèigè*	[yow jay-guh]
I don't want that	*Bú yào nèigè*	[boo yow nay-guh]
I want the receipt	*Yào fāpiào*	[yow fah-pee'ow]

Money

You will notice above that there is more than one way to refer to money and price:

Kuài	[kwai]	literally: pieces
Kuài qián	[kwai chee'en]	literally: pieces of money
Yuán	[yoo'an]	Yuan
Rénmínbì	[rem'in'bee]	RMB

In each case, just state the number followed by any of these terms.

This is 50 kuai	*Zhèi shì wǔ shí kuài*	[jay sh'r woo sh'r kwai]
120 Yuan	*Yī bǎi èr shí yuán*	[ee-bye ar-sh'r yoo'an]

Note that '*kuài*' and '*yuán*' are the most common.

10. The Most Common Questions and How to Answer Them

If you are in China for any length of time, you will notice a small number of questions which you are asked time and time again. This section will help you get through the beginnings of 90% of conversations with Chinese people you have just met!

1. **Where are you from?**   *Nǐ shì něi guó rén?*
2. **What's your name?**   *Nǐ jiào shénme míngzì?*
3. **How old are you?**   *Nǐ duō dà le?*
4. **Are you married?**   *Nǐ jiéhūn le ma?*
5. **Do you have children?**   *Nǐ yǒu háizǐ ma?*
6. **What do you do?**   *Nǐ yǒu shénme gōngzuò?*

1. Where are you from? – *Nǐ shì něi guó rén?*   [knee sh'r nay gwo(r) ren]

The simple formula to say where you are from is as follows:

I	am	(country)	person
Wǒ	*shì*	(…)	*rén*
[wo(r)	sh'r	(…)	ren]

e.g. *Wǒ shì Yīngguó rén. Nǐ shì Běijīng rén ma?*

A very short list of countries (If your country is not on here, just do a Google search for "Chinese dictionary", and then input your country to find the translation):

China	*Zhōng Guó*	[jong-gwo(r)]
England	*Yīng Guó*	[ying-gwo(r)]
Scotland	*Sū Gé Lán*	[soo-guh-lan]
Ireland	*Ài Ěr Lán*	[eye-er-lan]
USA	*Měi Guó*	[may-gwo(r)]
Canada	*Jiā Ná Dà*	[jah-nah-dah]
Australia	*Ào Dà Lì Yà*	[ow-dah-lee-yah]
New Zealand	*Xīn Xī Lán*	[shin-shee-lan]
Germany	*Dé Guó*	[duh-gwo(r)]
France	*Fǎ Guó*	[faah-gwo(r)]
Italy	*Yì Dà Lì*	[ee-dah-lee]
Spain	*Xī Bān Yá*	[shee-ban-yah]
Russia	*É Guó*	[uh-gwo(r)]

24

Do you speak … (language)?   *Nǐ shuō … ma?*

English	*Yīngwén, Yīng yǔ*	[ying-when, ying yew]
Chinese	*Zhōngwén, Hàn yǔ*	[jong-when, han yew]
French	*Fǎ yǔ*	[faah yew]
German	*Dé yǔ*	[duh yew]
Italian	*Yì dà lì yǔ*	[ee dah lee yew]
Spanish	*Xī bān yá yǔ*	[shee ban yah yew]
Russian	*É yǔ*	[uh yew]

I speak (a little)   *(Wǒ) shuō (yī diǎn diǎn)*
[wo(r) shwo(r) ee dee'en dee'en]

No, I can't speak it   *Bú huì shuō*   [boo hway shwo(r)]

25

2. **What's your name?** – *Nǐ jiào shénme míngzì?*
[knee jow shuh-muh ming-zuh]

My name's Peter	*Wǒ jiào Peter*	[wo(r) jow …]
What about you?	*Nǐ ne?*	[knee nuh]

3. **How old are you?** – *Nǐ duō dà le?* [knee dwo(r) dah luh]

I am (20)	*Wǒ (èr shí) suì*	[wo(r) ar sh'r sway]
What about you?	*Nǐ ne?*	[knee nuh]

4. **Are you married?** – *Nǐ jiéhūn le ma?* [knee j'yeh -huh+n luh ma]

Yes I am	*Jiéhūn le*	[j'yeh-huh+n luh]
No I'm not	*Méi yǒu*	[mayo]
This is my wife	*Zhèi shì wǒ de qī zǐ*	[jay sh'r wo(r) duh chee-dzuh]
This is my husband	*Zhèi shì wǒ de zhàng fū*	[jay sh'r wo(r) duh jahng foo]
I have a boyfriend	*Wǒ yǒu nán péng yǒu*	[wo(r) yo nan pung yo]
I have a girlfriend	*Wǒ yǒu nǚ péng yǒu*	[wo(r) yo new pung yo]

5. **Do you have children?** – *Nǐ yǒu háizǐ ma?* [knee yo hai-dzuh ma]

I have 2 children	*Yǒu liǎng gè hái zǐ*	[yo lee'ang-guh hai-dzuh]
1 son and 1 daughter	*Yīgè nán háizǐ hé yīgè nǚ háizǐ* [ee guh nan-hye-dzuh huh ee-guh new-hye-dzuh]	
I don't have children	*Méi yǒu háizǐ*	[mayo hai-dzuh]

6. What do you do? – *Nǐ yǒu shénme gōngzuò?* [knee yo shuh-muh gong-zwo(r)]

This is where you will have to look up your own occupation – Google "Chinese dictionary" and just type it in!

I am (an English teacher)   *Wǒ shì (Yīngyǔ lǎoshī)*
[wo(r) sh'r ying-yew lao-sh'r]

I am (a student)   *Wǒ shì (xué shēng)*
[wo(r) sh'r shway shung]

> **These 6 questions form the basis of most conversations you are likely to have with Chinese people you have just met!**

11. Chinese Tones

As previously mentioned, Chinese is a tonal language, meaning each word may be pronounced 4 different ways, giving different meanings (Remember too, that as was stated earlier, from the context you are speaking in, Chinese people can actually understand you without using the tones

The 4 different tones are as follows:

1st tone – Flat (e.g. mā – mother)
- Marked by a flat line above the syllable.
- It is higher than your normal pitch, and the tone is kept level (i.e. be careful not to let your tone fall, which is what naturally happens when you say a word in English).

2nd Tone – Rising (e.g. má – numb)
- Marked by a rising line (the French 'acute' accent) above the syllable.
This tone starts at your normal pitch and then rises.

3rd Tone – Falling then Rising (e.g. mǎ – horse)
- Marked by a line that falls then rises above the syllable.
- As it says, and starting at your normal pitch, this tone falls first, then rises.

4th Tone – Falling (e.g. mà – scold)
- Marked by a falling line (the French 'grave' accent) above the syllable.
- This tone starts higher than your normal pitch and falls to lower than your normal pitch.

Neutral Tone – Flat, no emphasis (e.g. ma – question word)
- This has no tone marking in the book, and is not strictly a tone, but rather 'no tone'.
- It is unemphasised and flat.

Listen Online

Rather than simply read the descriptions of the tones, you should try and listen to them online so that you can practice your own pronunciation.

To access the audio files for all the words & phrases in this book, please visit the following page:
http://www.mostbasiclanguages.com/#!most-basic-chinese-audio/c1yb8

The password for the page is:
mbcrecordings

Please enter the password when prompted, and if you have any problems, please email me to info@MostBasicLanguages.com and I will sort it out for you. Bear in mind too, that if you are visiting early, the audio files might not yet be available, but I aim to have them up there by the end of June 2013.

Regarding Chinese tones, there is also a lot available online – here is one good video where a guy gives the tones along with an opportunity for you to practise repeating after him (after watching, you can practise again with the words given above (the variations of *ma*):
http://www.youtube.com/watch?v=DGR2LTa2SlI

For those who wish to take this even further, this page also gives the further rules regarding tones, which involve changes when certain tones are followed by certain other tones. This is a bit more advanced, so is just for those who are interested:
http://www.trinity.edu/sfield/chin1501/ToneChange.html

If you wish to explore the subject further yourself, you can also just do a Google or Youtube search for 'Chinese tones' and you will find there are loads of pages, videos and audio files dealing with them.

Another great way to learn how the tones are really pronounced is from native speakers themselves, who are more than happy to help you with your pronunciation if you ask., and if you are staying for any length of time and want to become proficient at the language, then it is extremely easy to arrange a language exchange with any student, where you teach them English and they teach you Chinese – practising with a native speaker will greatly improve your pronunciation and everyday vocabulary. Alternatively, there are tons of places you can sign up for Chinese classes, which is really the best way to learn the language if you really want to become proficient.

12. A Summary of What You Will Need

In essence, this summary is simply reiterating the table of contents, but with slightly more detail. The intention is to highlight just how simple it is to build a working vocabulary in Chinese, which is sufficient to manage there for an extended period of time.

1. **Pronouns** – *wǒ, nǐ, tā* + *men, de*
2. **Verbs** – *yǒu, qù, yào* + *bú, ma*
3. **Nouns & Adjectives** – a bare minimum needed to get by – you will naturally pick up more when you are there.
4. **Other Useful Phrases** – these will add deeper levels of meaning to your conversation.
5. **Question Words** – *shénme, nǎ lǐ, shuí/shéi, wèi shénme, shénme shíhòu, zěnme.*
6. **Most Common Questions** – Answering these will help you survive many conversations.
7. **Numbers & Counting** – including stating how many, 1st, 2nd etc, telling the time.
8. **Situational Chinese** – in a taxi, in a restaurant, in a bar, in a shop.

13. Also Available

Please visit the Most Basic Languages website (mostbasiclanguages.com), where you will find the things outlined below (please note that if you are an early visitor, this is in the process of being expanded, and more is continually being added if you continue to check back). There is also a Facebook page, (https://www.facebook.com/pages/Most-Basic-Languages/176905519122610) where news of any free products will be posted.

Free Resources:
- I am trying to create and offer as many free resources as I can too. This will be notified via the Facebook page, and many resources will be available on Pinterest (http://pinterest.com/jimmcg1), which I am just in the process of getting going, including language resources, top restaurants and bars, top travel tips and top schools (for those emigrating), among other things.

- **Simplified Chinese characters** for "The Most Basic Chinese" – I acknowledged *Justin He* in the introduction, who has provided me with the tones that are now included for the Pinyin – he has also supplied me with the simplified Chinese characters for the words and phrases in this book – I assume most readers will not need this, and there is no place to put them in this book without it becoming too overbearing – however, if you are learning Chinese in depth and would also like the simplified Chinese characters, if you give me an email to: info@MostBasicLanguages.com, then I can send you them.

- **Audio files** for the words and phrases in this book are available at the following page, thanks again to *Justin He*, who kindly recorded them:

http://www.mostbasiclanguages.com/#!most-basic-chinese-audio/c1yb8

Password to access the page:
mbcrecordings

If you have any problems with these, then please send an email to info@MostBasicLanguages.com, and I will sort it out.

Phone Applications:
- At least one FREE app for every language covered. More are being designed and produced to be free.
- Other inexpensive apps designed to bring the easily accessible language of these books (The Most Basic _____).
- Further apps designed to enhance your language learning experience, including exercise books / apps to complement these books, as well as more apps to improve your travel experience.

Travel Apps & Books by Request:

If you have anything you would love to see in an app related to languages, travel or living abroad, or a specialized phrasebook of any kind, then simply send an email to info@mostbasiclanguages.com, and we will aim to have your app or book produced very quickly. It will then be made available cheaply for yourself and others to receive the benefits from.

*** This means that you can have any app or phrasebook you can think of to enhance your travel or language learning experience, within a short time of requesting it. ***

Other books:

- The Most Basic Language Series

All the basics needed to get by in a country, when travelling or living there. This series is being rapidly expanded to include more languages. The books included so far in this series are:
- The Most Basic Chinese – All You Need to Know to Get By
- The Most Basic Japanese – All You Need to Know to Get By
- The Most Basic Lithuanian – All You Need to Know to Get By
- The Most Basic Vietnamese – All You Need to Know to Get By

- The Most Vital Language Series

This is a series of short e-booklets, outlining days, dates and the vocabulary needed for staying in a hotel, and which I try to make **free** to download on Amazon on the 1st and 15th of each month. The books included so far in this series are:
- The Most Vital Chinese
- The Most Vital Vietnamese

More to come:

- More "**The Most Basic ___** " language books and apps to come. I am currently working with people on a number of other languages to expand the series, as well as converting the series into Android and IOS Applications which will also include the ability to listen to the pronunciation of a native speaker. Please keep an eye out for these in the near future if you are interested.

14. Final Note

As people in the West can sense, without ever having been there, China is an incredible country to visit, complex and intriguing, with fascinating ancient sites and interesting people.

If you have any desire or plans to travel or work in China, then knowing at least the simple language presented in this booklet will greatly enhance your experience, as you are enabled to socialise with the locals and get to know what the people are really like.

In fact, as anyone who has already visited China knows, it is one of the few large countries left where you simply cannot get by without speaking the language. In addition, the locals sincerely appreciate foreigners making an effort to converse with them in Chinese, and it also goes a long way with bargaining for prices!

So my advice is to make this small effort to learn a little of the language, and you will find a whole new dimension has been added to your trip!

Also, if you would like any advice on travelling to China, feel free to email me at info@mostbasiclanguages.com, and if I can help in any way, I will.

Made in the USA
Lexington, KY
21 October 2014